This journal belongs to

Benjamin AKA BAB
Archibald
Derserra

HOW TO TRAIN YOUR DRAGON

A Journal for Heroes

KEEP OUT

CRESSIDA COWELL

LITTLE, BROWN AND COMPANY
New York   Boston

Text and illustrations copyright
© 2014 by Cressida Cowell

Little, Brown and Company

Hachette Book Group
1290 Avenue of the Americas, New York, NY 10104
Visit us at lb-kids.com

Little, Brown and Company is a division of Hachette Book Group, Inc.
The Little, Brown name and logo are trademarks of Hachette Book Group, Inc.

The publisher is not responsible for websites (or their content) that are not owned by the publisher.

First U.S. Edition: November 2015
Originally published in Great Britain in 2014 by Hodder Children's Books

ISBN 978-0-316-30743-7

10 9 8 7 6 5 4 3 2 1

RRD-C

Printed in the United States of America

"The past is another land, and we cannot go to visit. So if I say there were dragons, and men rode upon their backs, who alive has been there, and can tell me that I'm wrong?"

SPRING
WETTINGS

"I was not a natural at the heroism business. I had to work at it. This is the story of becoming a Hero the Hard Way."

Hiccup Horrendous Haddock the Third

TOOTHLESS,
Hiccup's disobedient little
dragon

↑
This is Toothless, in a hibernation sleep.

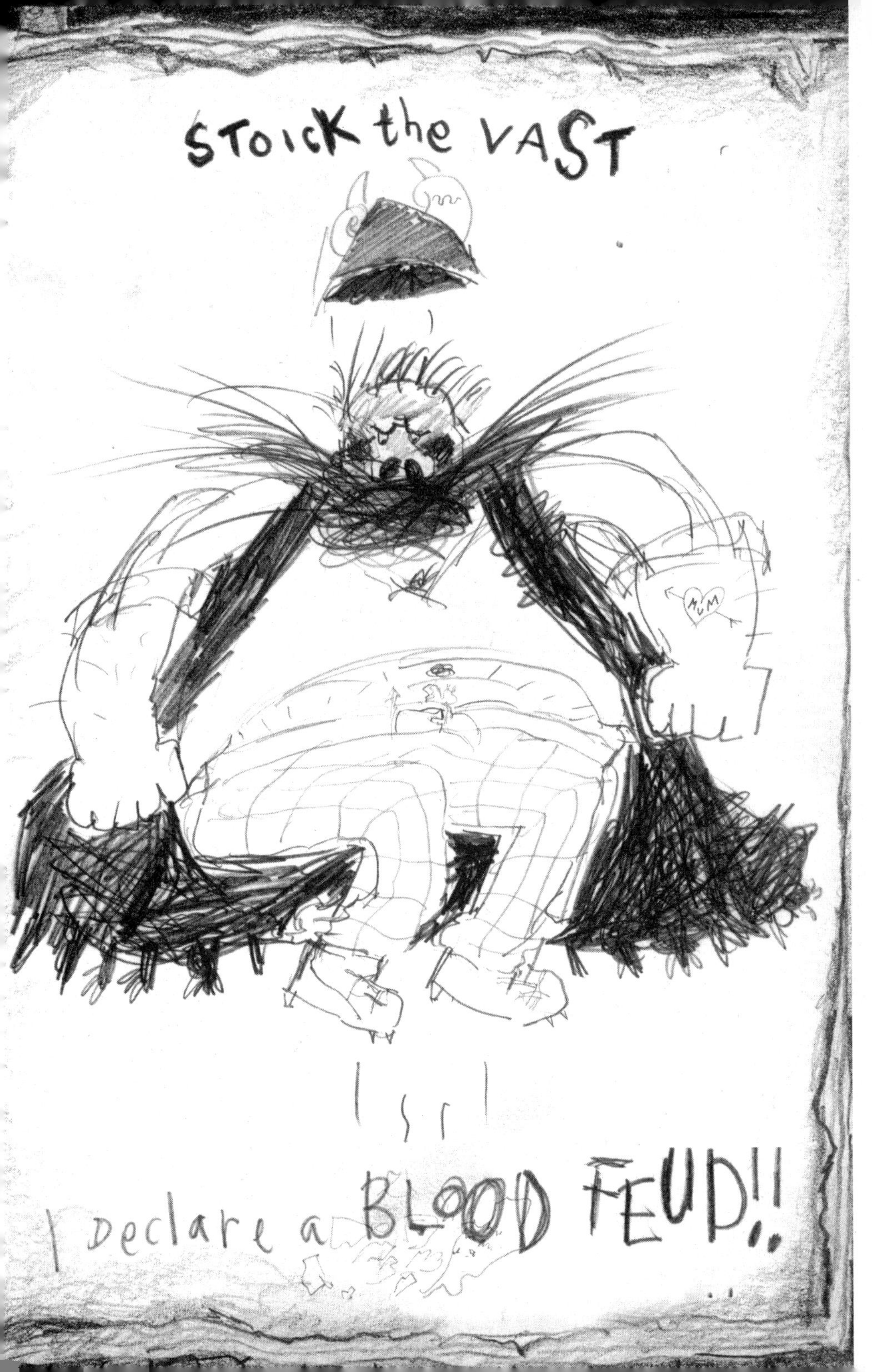
STOICK the VAST
MUM
I Declare a BLOOD FEUD!!

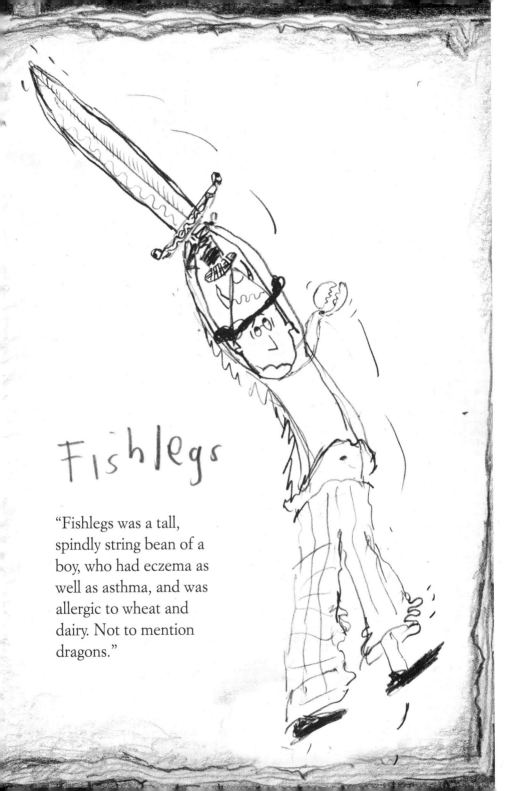

Fishlegs

"Fishlegs was a tall, spindly string bean of a boy, who had eczema as well as asthma, and was allergic to wheat and dairy. Not to mention dragons."

SOME FIERY DRAGON JOKES:

Q: What's as big as a Seadragonus Giganticus Maximus but weighs nothing?
A: Its shadow!

Q: What do you call a deaf Driller Dragon?
A: Anything you like—he can't hear you!

Q: What do you find inside Wartihog's clean nose?
A: Fingerprints!

Q: What do Stoick the Vast, Mogadon the Meathead, and Baggybum the Beerbelly all have in common (besides bad breath and excessive sweating)?
A: They all have the same middle name!

Q: What's the best way to catch a Basic Brown dragon?
A: Have someone throw it at you.

Q: How do Vikings send secret messages?
A: By Norse code!

Q: How do you know when a Seadragonus Giganticus Maximus is under your bed?
A: When your nose hits the ceiling.

Q: What do you get when a Sniffer Dragon sneezes?
A: Out of the way!

One day the great god Thor decided to come down to Earth and challenge Thwettibot the Hero to a rock-lifting contest. After a day of lifting rocks, Thwettibot conceded defeat. "You did well!" said the god graciously. "For I am Thor." "You're Thor?" said Thwettibot. "Lithen, Mithter, I'm tho thore, I can barely thtand up!"

Camicazi

"The indomitable Heir to the Bog-Burglar Tribe, whose hair looks like it has been vigorously back-combed by squirrels."

Camicazi riding her Rocket Ripper, Typhoon, very low over the Murderous Mountains.

"He was a seven-foot giant with a mad glint in his one working eye and a beard like exploding fireworks."

"We're all snatching precious moments from the peaceful jaws of time."

Old Wrinkly

"There's no such thing as im-POSSIBLE, Hiccup," snorted Old Wrinkly. "Only im-PROBABLE. The only thing that limits us are the limits to our imaginations."

NOT THE SETTLING KIND

An Old Viking Archipelago song

I have never cared for castles
or a crown that grips too tight.
Let the night sky be my starry roof,
and the moon my only light.

My heart was born a Hero,
my storm-bound sword won't rest,
I left the Harbor long ago
on a never-ending Quest.

I am off to the horizon,
where the wild wind blows the foam.
Come get lost with me, Love,
and the sea shall be our home.

take this ruby as a token of my love, I promise you....

I will return,

TRUE LOVE

My one true love vanished,
and my heart broke that day.
But once you've loved truly,
Thor, then you know the way!

Once I loved truly, Thor,
and my heart paid the price.
Let me love truly, Thor,
let me love **TWICE**!

"We listened hard, for what mothers say to their babies when they are about to be parted—well, that is worth listening to."

"And as small and quiet and unimportant as our fighting may look, perhaps we might all work together…and break out of the prisons of our own making. Perhaps we might be able to keep this fierce and beautiful world of ours as free for all of us as it seemed to be on that blue afternoon of my childhood."

Snotface Snotlout

(Hiccup's unpleasant cousin)

"Hiccup will not be leading this group, because HE is not a leader. I am."

Does this look like the sort of dragon who would poo in a helmet?

Toothless doing a poo in Alvin's helmet

Conversations with Toothless

Dinnertime...

Toothless: Issa yuck-yuck.
This is disgusting.

Toothless: Me na likeit di stinkfish. Issa yuck-yuck.
Issa poo-poo. Issa doubly doubly yuck-yuck.
I don't like haddock. It's disgusting. It's gross. It's really disgusting.

You: Okey dokey so questa yow eaty?
All right then, so what will you eat?

Toothless: Me eaty di miaowla...
I want to eat the cat...

You: (you can raise your voice now) NA EATY
DI BUM-SUPPORT, NA EATY DI SLEEPY-SLAB, PLUS
DOUBLY DOUBLY NA EATY DI MIAOWLA!
Don't eat the chair, don't eat the bed, and definitely don't eat the cat!

Bath Time...

When a dragon has spent the whole day in a mud pit, and they then want to curl up in your bed, you have no option: YOU HAVE TO GIVE THEM A BATH. 'Good luck.

Toothless: Me na wash di bum. Me na wash di face. Me na wash di claws. Me na splishy oo di splashy ATALL.
I do not want a bath.

You are going to have to be cunning and use PSYCHOLOGY.

You: Na bathtime ever never ever never.
Me repeeti. Na bathtime EVER NEVER.
On no account are you to get in the bath.

Toothless (whining): Me wanti splishy splashy.
I want a bath.

You: Okey dokey just wun time.
All right just this once.

Hoody drunken di bath juice?
Who has drunk up the bath water?

SUMMER
BOILINGS

"Humungously Hotshot the Hero was as cool as a cat, twirling his whiskers on a freshly frozen iceberg…"

And spare
a thought
for those

THE Hairy Scary Librarian

"You, dear reader, I am sure cannot imagine what it might be like to live in a world in which books are banned.

For surely such things will never happen in the future?

Thank Thor that you live in a time and a place where people have the right to live and think and write and read their books in peace, and there are no need for Heroes any-more…"

who have not been so LUCKY.

SOME MORE FIERY DRAGON JOKES:

Q: What has six eyes, six arms, six legs, three heads, and a very short life?
A: Three people about to be eaten by a Tongue-twister.

Q: How do you know if there is an Eight-Legged Battlegore in your refrigerator?
A: The door won't shut!

Q: What's the nickname for someone who put their right hand in the mouth of a Darkbreather?
A: Lefty.

Q: How do you best raise a baby dragon?
A: With a crane.

Q: Why did the Raptortongue cross the road?
A: To eat the chickens on the other side.

Q: What game does the Giant Bee-Eater like to play with humans?
A: Squash.

Q: What is the best thing to do if you see an Exterminator dragon?
A: Pray that it doesn't see you.

Q: Where did the teacher send the Viking when he got sick in class?
A: To the school Norse.

Q: Why was the greedy person like a Viking?
A: Because he ate like a Norse!

Q: Why can't Vikings play cards on their longboats?
A: Because they're always sitting on the deck.

Q: What do you get if you cross a stink dragon with a flower?
A: I don't know, but I'm sure not going to smell it.

Q: How does a Pricklepine play leapfrog?
A: Very carefully!

Song of the

NANODRAGON

(while licking off honey)

O Human Fatness who tried to eat me,
Great Wobbling Vomit of Repulsive Man-Flesh,
I cannot kill you NOW,
Though I would like to,
But you will regret this, Blubber-Man.
You will regret this in the quiet darkness of the nighttime,
For I have friends.
I have friends who will itch you into nightmares.
Their feet will plow your skin into rashes,
And you will sleep no more, O Stomach-with-a-Head-on-It
You will sleep no more.

O Balloon of Lard who tried to eat me,
Man Uglier than an Exploded Jellyfish,
I cannot kill you NOW,
Though I would like to,
But I can wait, Flesh-Dangler.
I can wait, ticking in the corner like Fate.
And I have friends,
I have friends who will crawl with me into your coffin,
Where you are lying, hoping for the quiet sleep of death.
And we will eat YOU, O Sad Lump of Man Meat,
We will eat you.

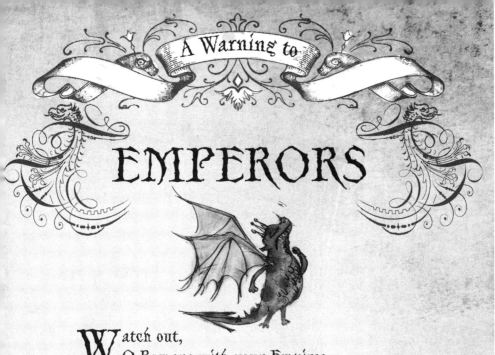

A Warning to

EMPERORS

Watch out,
O Romans with your Empires
And your Stinking Breath.
Watch out for the smaller things of this world,
For we are going to get you...one day.
You live your lives up in the skies,
Building your aqueducts and your coliseums,
And you never think of US,
Buzzing away in the grasses.
But we see you,
And if you bend your ear you just might hear
The steady beat of countless feet that come to eat.
The wall that curls a hundred miles across a continent,
That temple built with the tears of millions of slaves,
And all your most mighty and splendid creations
Shall turn to dust in our mouths.
So watch out,
O Caesars with Fat Bottoms and Hard Hearts,
Watch out.

WE WILL
FIGHT THEM
ON THE BEACHES!
WE WILL FIGHT
THEM IN THE BRACKEN!
WE WILL FIGHT THEM
IN THOSE BOGGY,
MARSHY BITS THAT
ARE SO DIFFICULT TO
WALK THROUGH WITHOUT
LOSING YOUR SHOES!
WE WILL
NEVER
SURRENDER!

West

East

for
Hiccup
and the
Dragonmark

for
Alvin
and the
Witch

Which way would
Snotlout Go?

Conversations with Toothless

In the Middle of the Night...

I am very hungry

Me has b-b-buckets di belly-scream.
I am very hungry.

Me isna burped si ISSA middling o di zuzztime.
I don't care if it IS the middle of the night.

Me needy di grubbings SNIP-SNAP!
I want food RIGHT NOW!

Oo mes'll do di yowlyshreekers too fortissimo theys'll earwig me indi BigManGaff.
Or I'll scream so loudly they'll hear me in Valhalla.

Me needy di S-S-S-S-SALTSICKS.
I want OYSTERS.

Yow g-g-grabba di saltsicks low indi Landscoop. Sna staraway.
You can get oysters from the Harbor. It's not far.

M-m-me gogo ta yowlshreek...
I'm starting to scream...

(three quarters of an hour later)

Yow me p-p-peepers undo!
You woke me up!

Wah is DA?
What is THAT?

Da na goggle com s-s-saltsicks...
That doesn't look like oysters...

THAT looks like bogeys.

DA goggle com sniffersludge...
THAT looks like bogeys...

Sniffersludge p-p-plus di squidink tiddles...
Bogeys with black bits in them...

Me no likeit di squidink tiddles. Issa y-y-yuck-yuck.
I don't like black bits. They're disgusting.

Watever, me is tow zuzzready por di scrumming.
Anyway, I'm too tired to eat.

Mes'll zip di peepers.
I'm going to sleep.

"Old Wrinkly named it Endeavor. He said the name was important, because 'to endeavor' means trying to do something even when you know you might be beaten before you even start."

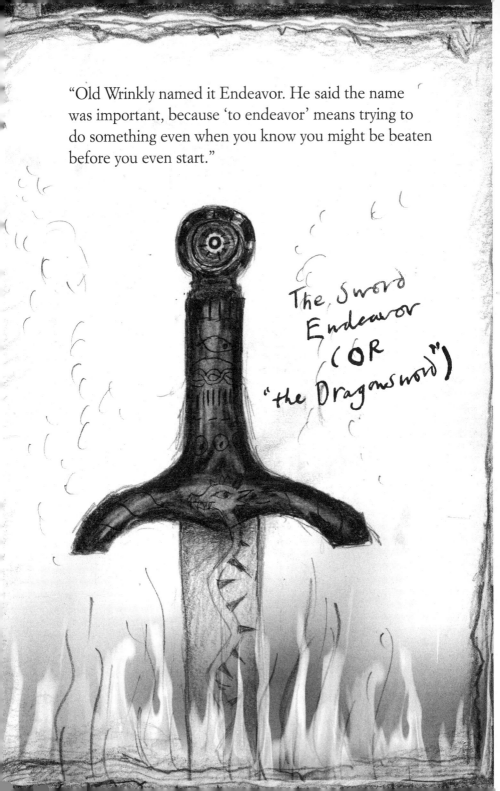

The Sword
Endeavor
(OR
"the Dragonsword")

Watch and learn,
my boy. Watch
and learn.

"You do not have to accept the hand that Fate has dealt you. Look at me, the skinniest, most unlikely Viking ever, now known as this great Hero all around the world."

the
DARK SIDE of THE AXE
(a moving little lullaby)

Come and dance the Deathwalk
Beneath the grinning moon...
We'll do the dance together
In the dying afternoon...

The Deathwalk looks so tricky,
But I think you'll learn it quick,
Just step into my axe's arms,
She'll teach you in a tick...

See the jolly skeletons,
A-dancing on the seal
They haven't got no cares how
Not like you and me...
They went and did the
DEATHWALK
That crazy hightime
beat...

And now they partner ghosts and whales
On bony, pearly felt...

"Now all those who had laughed had watched him as he swam, entirely unaided, up the whole length of the bay. Even though he was so tired he could barely put one foot in front of the other, his back was straight, his head held high."

A proud moment for Fishlegs

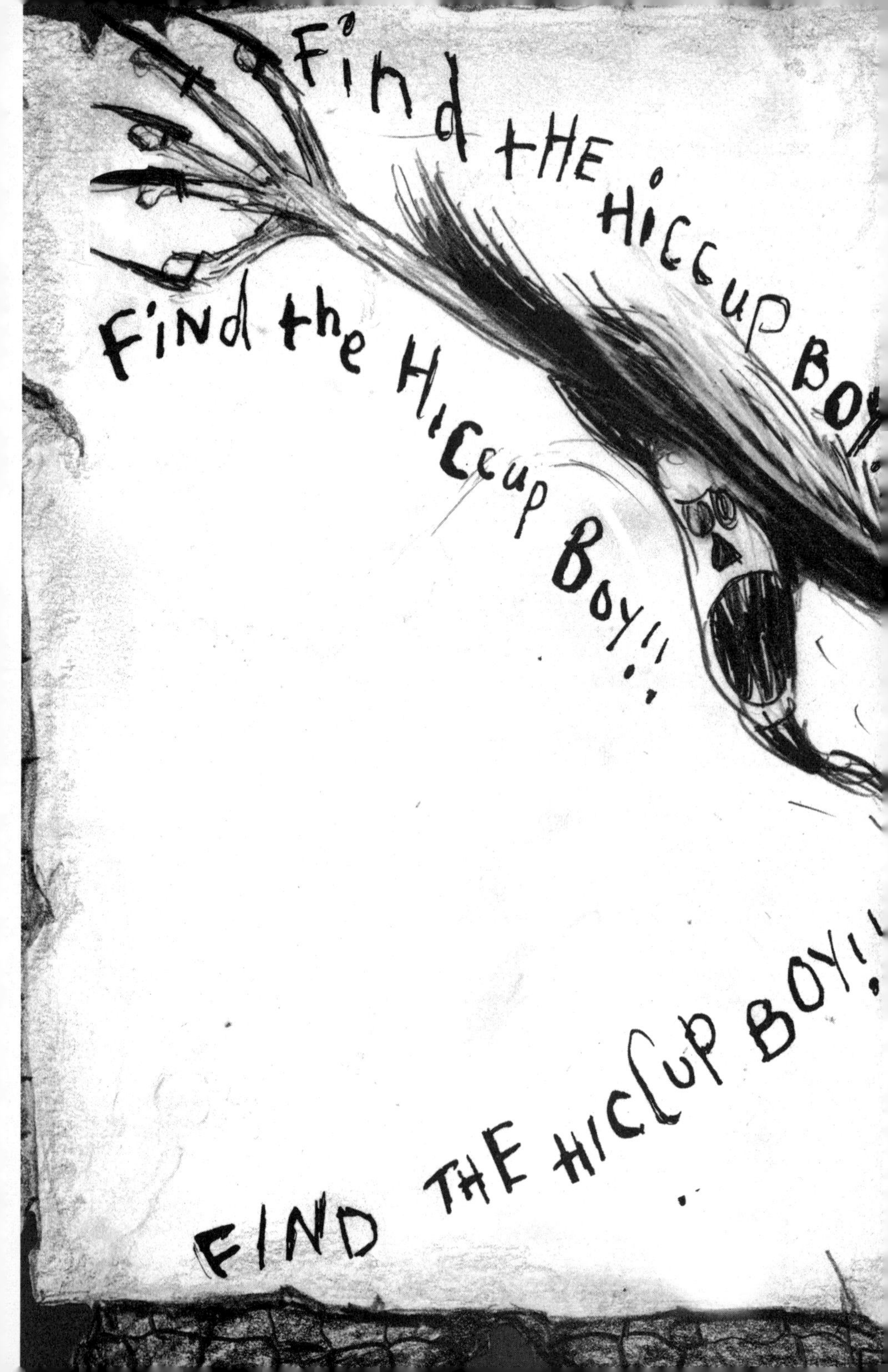
Find tHE HICCUP BOY
Find the HICCUP BOY!!
FIND THE HICCUP BOY!!

The Witch Excellinor,
a particularly unpleasant
and Scary witch

You
Can't
keep a
BOG-BURGLAR
UNDER
LOCK
AND
KEY!

Conversations with Toothless

Toilet Training...

You: Toothless, ta COGLET me wantee ta cack-cack in di greenclaw crapspot...
Toothless, you KNOW I want you to poo in the dragon toilets...

Toothless: O yessee, yessee, me coglet...
Yes, yes, I know...

You (pointing at large poo in the middle of Stoick's bed): Erg...questa SA?
So what, then, is THIS?

PAUSE

Toothless (hopefully): Ummm...un chocklush snik-snak?
Er...a chocolate cookie?

You: Snotta chocklush snik-snak, issa CACK-CACK, issa cack-cack di Toothless, NA in di greenclaw crapspot, may oopla bang splosh in di middling di sleepy-slab di pappa.
This isn't a chocolate cookie, it's a POO, it's one of YOUR poos, Toothless, and it ISN'T in the dragon toilets, it's right bang splat in the middle of my father's bed.

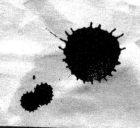

YET MORE FIERY DRAGON JOKES:

Q: What's big, heavy, dangerous, and has sixteen wheels?
A: A Riproarer on roller skates.

Q: Where does a three-ton dragon sit?
A: Anywhere it likes.

A policeman stopped a man who was walking along with a Driller Dragon and ordered him to take it to the zoo at once.
The next day the policeman saw the same man, still with the Driller Dragon.
"I thought I told you to take that dragon to the zoo," he said.
"I did," said the man, "and now I'm taking him to the movies."

Q: What steps do you take if a Triple-Headed Rageblast is coming toward you?
A: Big ones!

Q: What do you get if you cross a glowworm with a python?
A: A fifteen-foot strip light who will strangle you to death!

Q: What time did the Saber-Toothed Driver Dragon go to the dentist?
A: Tooth hurty.

Q: What do you call a dragon who is good at rhyming?
A: A rap-tile.

Q: What do you say to a lazy Gronckle?
A: Stop dragon your tail!

FUNNY!

F-F-funny

funny!

clap.
clap
clap.
clap

Q: What do dragons do on their birthday?
A: They have to blow on their cake to light the candles.

Q: How was the Viking able to afford such an expensive ship?
A: It was on sail!

Q: What dragon can jump higher than the Great Hall?
A: All of them! Great Halls can't jump!

AUTUMN
FALLINGS

"Hiccup's mother is a great Hero who is often away Questing."

THree cheers foR ValHallarama.

THE DRAGON BRACELET

"It is a constant reminder to me of the human ability to create something beautiful even when things are at their darkest.

I have worn that bracelet every day of my life."

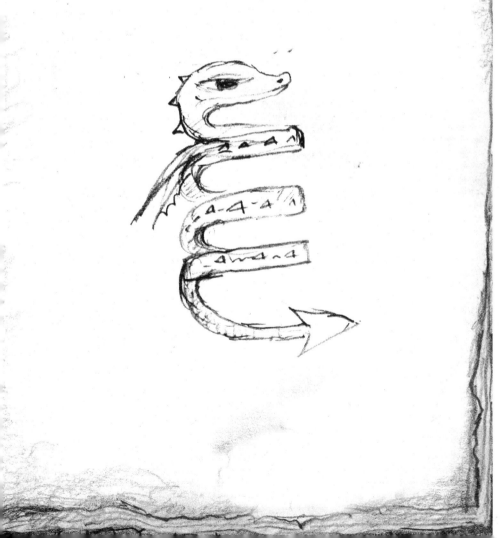

I DIDN'T MEAN TO COME HERE

The Hooligan Tribal Anthem, composed by Hiccup's ancestor Great Hairybottom

I didn't mean to come here…

And I didn't mean to stay…

It's just where the sea wind blew me

One accidental day…

I was on my way to America,

But I took a left turn at the Pole,

And I lost my shoe in a rainy bog,

Where my heart got stuck in the hole…

It wasn't where I meant to be,

And it wasn't where I had my start,

But now I'll never leave these rain-soaked bogs

Because Berk is where I left my heart!

"I DIDN'T MEAN TO COME HE-ERE..
NO, I DIDN'T MEAN TO STA-A-AY...
BUT I LOST MY HEART TO THESE RAINY BOGS,
AND I'LL NE-E-E-VER GO AW-A-AY!!"

I didn't mean to come here,
And I didn't mean to STAY;
It's just where the sea wind BLEW ME
ONE ACCIDENTAL DAY,
WHAT A HERO!!

ropes for climbing and swinging on

← knapsack for burgled items

things for picking locks

← lots of secret pockets

sword

protective goggles

← tiny dagger for emergencies

spiked shoes for extra GRIP

Camicazi's Burglary Equipment

ADVANCED BURGLARY TIPS from CAMICAZI

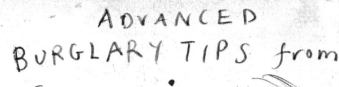

Burgling from Grabbit the Grim

fig 1.

Gently remove his helmet, approaching from <u>above</u>.

A steady hand is essential for all burglary exercises. Quick wits are as important as nimble fingers, as demonstrated HERE:

fig 2.

Softly remove swords and sandals, approaching from <u>below</u>.

If you get caught SHEEP-RUSTLING: ACT SURPRISED.

"Oh my goodness! You're right, there IS a sheep on my head! Well, I have ABSOLUTELY NO IDEA how *that* could have gotten there..."

fig 3. Your victim realizes he has been BURGLED.

A quick getaway is ALWAYS a good idea...

EVEN MORE DRAGON JOKES:

A race is about to start. Gobber shouts
"1...2...3...GO!" and blows the whistle. Everybody
except Clueless runs.
GOBBER: Clueless! Why aren't you running?
CLUELESS: Because my number is 4!

Q: Where do Viking warriors keep their armies?
A: Up their sleevies!

Q: What does a Seadragonus Giganticus Maximus eat?
A: Fish and ships.

Q: Why does Hiccup take a pencil to bed?
A: So he can draw the curtains.

Q: Why did the Rhinoback cross the road?
A: Because it was the chicken's day off.

Q: What do you find in the middle of dragons?
A: The letter g!

"Sometimes it is only a true friend who knows what we mean when we try to speak. Somebody who has spent a lot of time with us, listens carefully to what we are trying to say, and tries to understand.

Fishlegs understood."

We must
be STRONG,
Fishlegs. We
must hope
for the
BEST!

He would be strong.
He would hope
for the best.

"Sometimes time cannot tick backward.
Sometimes you cannot put a dragon back in a forest,
nor a witch back in a tree trunk, nor the breath back
into a friend when all the breath has gone.
War really does have terrible consequences."

"A Hero is FOREVER."

Conversations with Toothless

Toothless's Guide to Being P-p-polite...

Moo-lady, yow snoddly sniffer is giganticus plus warticus—plus warra eye-pleezee, fur-sprouty hug-dangles!

Madam, you have a very large and lovely spotty nose—and what beautiful hairy arms!

Toothless issa griefspotty me misschance f-f-flicka-flame ta gob-sprout. Twassa bigtime hiccup.

I am so sorry that I accidentally set fire to your beard. It was a total mistake.

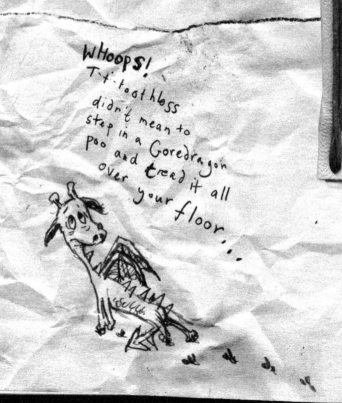

WHOOPS!
T-t-toothless didn't mean to step in a Goredragon poo and tread it all over your floor...

Toothless mak ta me m-m-most speshally griefspotties. Toothless's runners pop in a cack-cack di Goredragon, plus me pressit muchwide ondi floorsheet.

I give you my most heartfelt apologies. I seem to have stepped in Goredragon poo and got it all over your carpet.

T-t-toothless goggla ta struggla wi munch-munch di saltsicks lonelywise. Teggly me adda.

I can see you are having trouble eating all those oysters on your own. Let me help you.

Ne-ah, Toothless na s-s-sporta da sprouty-warm. Ta maka me inta un girly-goo, plus me preffa ma flame-shootys coldover and me flip-flaps lendinta forkfreezies.

Thankee par ta warmwishes.

No, I will NOT wear that furry coat. It makes me look like a sissy, and I would rather my fire-holes freeze up and my wings turn into ice pops. Thank you for your concern.

The Murderous Tribe did not often receive visitors.

HEROIC SWORDFIGHTING TIPS

The Hypnotizing switcheroo.

Make sure you do not confuse YOURSELF.

The old "I do it better blindfolded," feel-the-Force trick

HEROIC SWORDFIGHTING TIPS

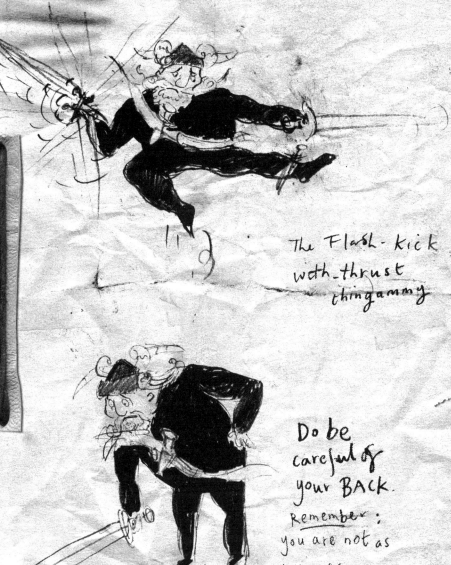

The Flash-kick
with-thrust
thingammy

Do be
careful of
your BACK.
Remember:
you are not as
young as you were.

"Of course humans and dragons can live together!" said Hiccup fiercely. "Some of my best friends are dragons! It's just that things have gone wrong somehow…The dragons have become enslaved when they ought to be free. But you HAVE to believe that people and dragons can be better. You HAVE to believe in a better world…"

Song of the Singing Supper

Watch me, Great Destroyer,
as I settle down to lunch.
Killer whales are tasty 'cause they've
got a lot of crunch.

Great white sharks are scrumptious,
but here's a little tip:
Those teeny-weeny pointy teeth can
give a nasty nip...

Humans can be bland,
but if you have some salt on hand,
A little bit of brine,
will make them taste div-I-I-I-ne...

I tell the mighty big blue whale
his life is over soon.
With one swish of this armored tail
I put out the sun and moon...

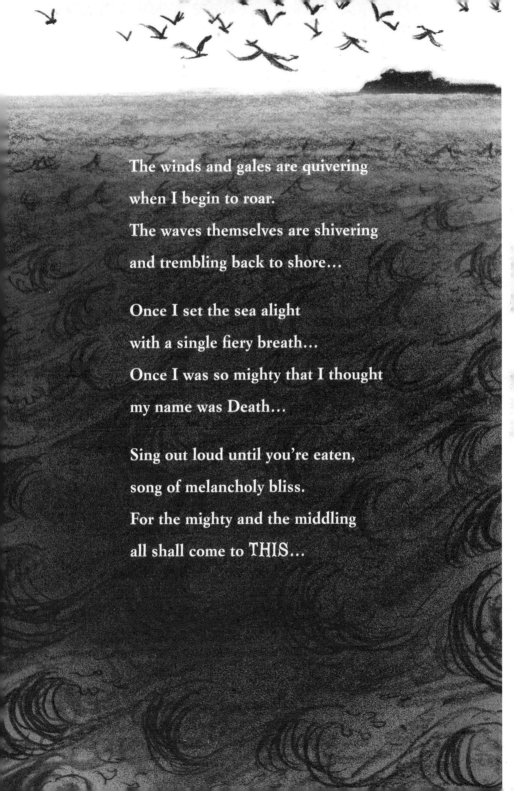

The winds and gales are quivering
when I begin to roar.
The waves themselves are shivering
and trembling back to shore...

Once I set the sea alight
with a single fiery breath...
Once I was so mighty that I thought
my name was Death...

Sing out loud until you're eaten,
song of melancholy bliss.
For the mighty and the middling
all shall come to THIS...

"I WILL NEVER GIVE UP FIGHTING YOU, WITCH!"

"You see, it was not only Hiccup who was growing up, it was the entire world around him—and when whole worlds grow up, that can be painful and difficult."

"Trust me, if you train your dragon the Hard Way, you will develop an unshakable and lifelong bond…Eventually."

STILL MORE DRAGON JOKES:

Q: Why did Hiccup's music teacher need a ladder?
A: To reach the high notes.

"Mom, can we have a dragon for Christmas?"
"Certainly not, you'll have turkey like everybody else."

Q: How do you get down off a dragon?
A: You don't. You get down off a duck.

Q: What did the policeman say to the Triple-Header Rageblaster?
A: Hello, Hello, Hello.

Q: What do you get if you cross a Raptortongue with a dog?
A: A very nervous postman.

Q: Why don't Vampire Dragons have many friends?
A: Because they're a pain in the neck.

Q: Why was the glowworm unhappy?
A: Because her children were not very bright.

Teacher: How do you spell *Electricsquirm*?
Dogsbreath the Duhbrain: E-L-E-K-T-R-I-K-S-K-W-O-R-M
Teacher: That's not how the dictionary spells it!
Dogsbreath the Duhbrain: You didn't ask me how the dictionary spelled it!

T-t-tell Toothless another one please please please

WINTER
FREEZINGS

Dragon Hibernation

Most dragons hibernate in the winter. Big ones go in a cave, but smaller ones dig themselves a hole to sleep in, and the deeper the hole, the colder the winter will be.

← A Common or Garden dragon hibernating for the winter.

Some dragons, like Saber-Toothed Driver Dragons, do not hibernate at all, and they are called Evergreens, and this is a funny name for them because Saber-Toothed Driver Dragons are always white.

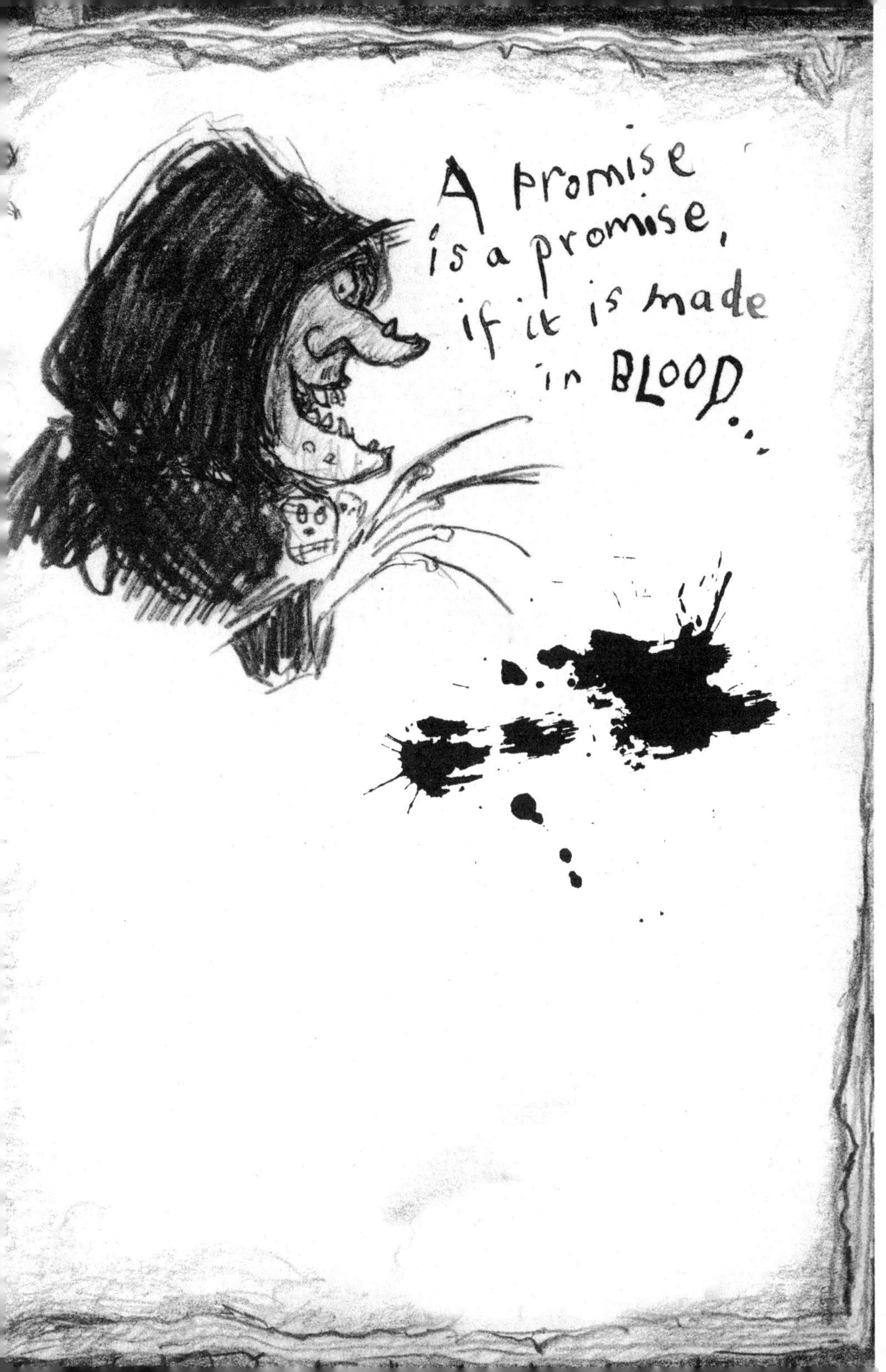
A promise
is a promise,
if it is made
in BLOOD...

"The Hero cares not for a WILD
Winter's STORM
For it CARRIES Him SWIFT
ON THE BACK OF THE STORM
ALL MAY BE LOST AND
OUR HEARTS MAY BE WORN
BUT
A HERO FIGHTS FOREVER!"

"UP with your SWORD and STRIKE at the GALE,
RIDE the rough SEAS for those WAVES are your HOME
WINTER'S MAY FREEZE but our HEARTS do not FAIL,
...HOOLIGAN...HEARTS...FOREVER!!!"

"STRONG are the BREASTS that CRUSH WITHOUT FEAR, MIGHTY the PLAITS that can STRANGLE the WIND, NIM-BLE THE FINGERS that BUR-GLE the BOG, BOG-BURGLARS...STAND...TOGETHER !!!"

I say
NO!
Dragons
and humans
should
be FREE!

"Most of us are lucky not to be Kings and Heroes, because we do not have to make the choices Kings and Heroes have to make."

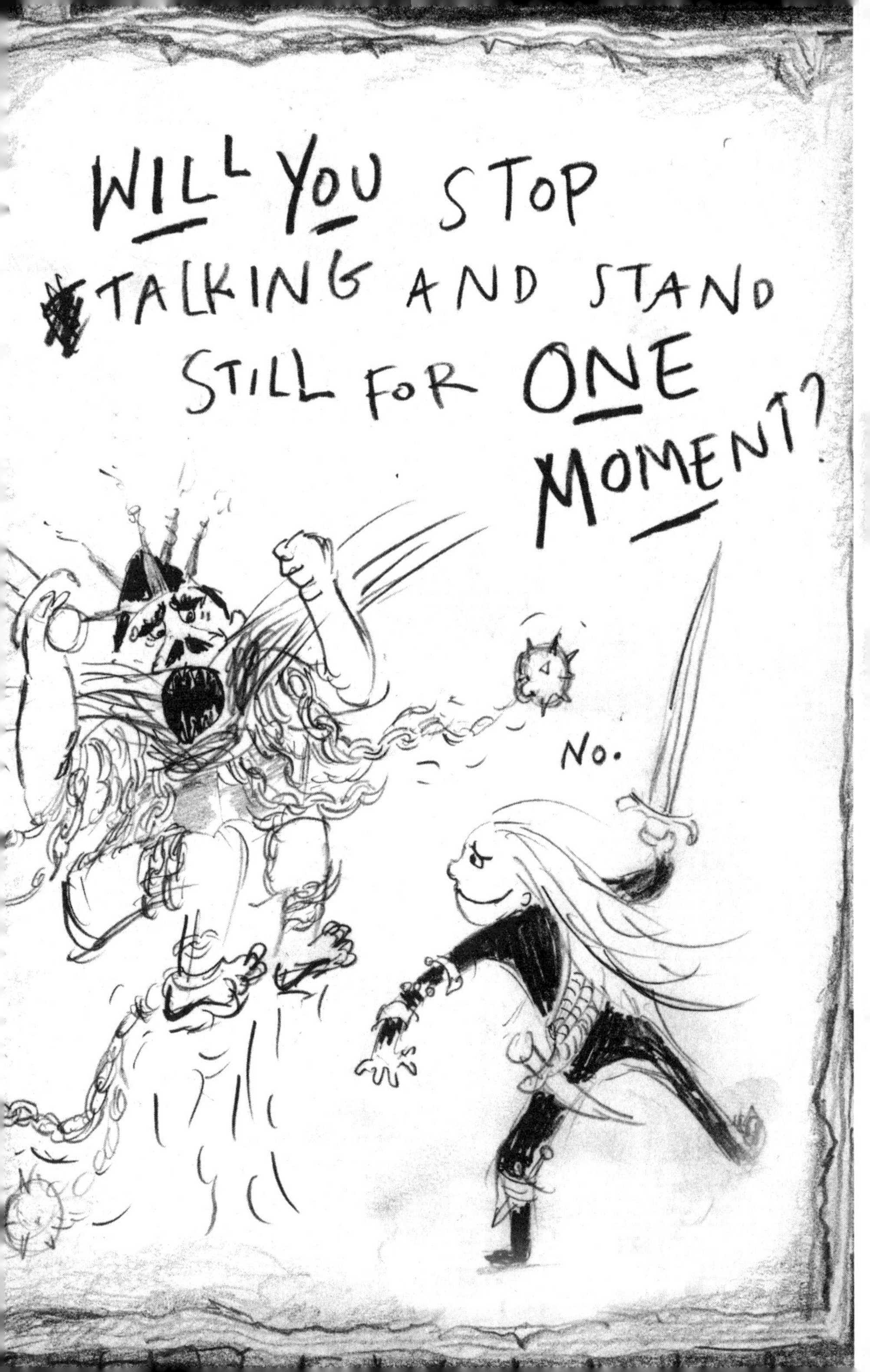
WILL YOU STOP TALKING AND STAND STILL FOR ONE MOMENT?
NO.

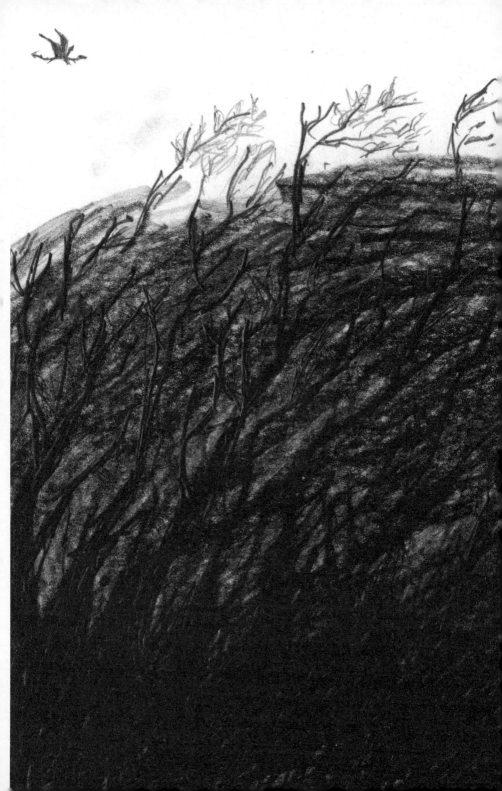

"However small we are, we should all fight for what we believe to be right. And I don't mean fight with the power of our fists or the power of our swords...

I mean the power of our brains and our thoughts and our dreams."

FISHLEGS'S GUIDE ON HOW NOT TO SKI

Fig 1.
Wobble forward,
knees bent, bottom
out, determined
expression on face.

Fig 2. Whoops!
Slight ski crossover
balance situation...

FISHLEGS'S GUIDE ON HOW NOT TO SKI

Fig 3.

Fall over.

Fig 4.

It is
VERY IMPORTANT

to learn how
to STOP.

"A beautiful little island, all lit up under a canopy of stars. Maybe it was a little rainier on Berk than you might wish for. Perhaps it was a bit on the windy, boggy, rocky, and heathery side. No doubt there were lands with bluer skies and richer soils somewhere over the horizon. But Berk was the Hooligans' home, and perhaps that is what really matters after all."

Conversations with Toothless

Dragon Rivalry...

Your dragon can feel a little threatened when a new
dragon enters the household. Be patient and he will get
over it. Hopefully...

Toothless: Hogfly ne-ah com sweetie-giggly com T-t-toothless.
The Hogfly is NOT as cute as Toothless.

You: Simple ne-ah, Toothless. TOOTHLESS si la Mos Xcellent
Oos. May noos ava be keenalee a di fella.
*Of course not, Toothless. TOOTHLESS is the Best One. But we
have to be nice to him.*

Toothless: Simply, simply. Toothless willa be B-B-BIGTIME
keenalee a di stupidissimo lacksmart greenblood.
Of course, of course. Toothless will be VERY nice.

Pause.

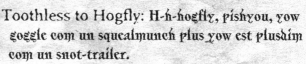

Toothless to Hogfly: H-h-hogfly, pishyou, yow
goggle com un squealmunch plus yow est plusdim
com un snot-trailer.
*Hogfly, please, you look like a pig, and you are
more stupid than a snail.*

You: TOOTHLESS!
TOOTHLESS!

Toothless (whining): May Toothless speekee pishyou!
But Toothless said please!

Another pause.

Toothless: Hogfly, yow wantee a play hidey-plus-looky?
Y-y-yow hide oppsthere wi di keendlee ickle Wettingsgreenblood,
undi Noddle-Scratchers, plus me adda a ponder o
marvels und cum opps und loc yow...
*Hogfly, do you want to play hide-and-seek?
You hide out there and play with the sweet
little Sea-Dragon and the Brainpickers, and I'll
count to a hundred million and then I'll come
out and find you...*

Hogfly (tail wagging happily): Woof!
Woof!

H-h-hogfly
NOT as
Cute as
Toothless

Time cannot
be fought.

"There is nothing more painful than watching an old lion lose a fight, particularly to his own son."

This Quest is now within our grasp.

"Was it all worth the Archipelago in flames? I do not know; you decide."

"Join the Red-Rage and REBEL,
Make red your claws with human blood,
Obliterate the Human Filth ...
Torch the HUMANS like a wood ...
The Rebellion is coming. :

"JOIN tHE RED-RAGE and Rebel,
Brother-DRAGONS, rebel!"

"Slake your thirst with human tears,
Do not spare the human child,
Incinerate the human pest,
The Dragontime is Coming."

THE LAST FEW DRAGON JOKES:

Q: Why did Gobber throw butter out the window?
A: Because he wanted to see butter fly.

Q: Where do tough dragons come from?
A: Hard-boiled eggs.

Q: How do you know if you've had a dragon in your fridge?
A: Footprints in the butter.

Q: Why don't Vikings like long fairy tales?
A: They tend to dragon.

Q: Why did the dragon spit out the clown?
A: Because he tasted funny.

Q: What is green and has four legs and two trunks?
A: Two seasick tourists!

Q: How do Vampire Dragons keep their breath smelling nice?
A: They use extractor fangs!

Q: Where do you find nanodragons?
A: It depends on where you lost them.

A Viking went into a cafe with a Doomfang. They ordered lots and lots of food and drinks and stuffed their faces. This went on for about two hours when suddenly the Doomfang fell over dead on the floor. The Viking put his coat and helmet on, left some money on the table, and started to walk out. "Hey," said the cafe owner, "you can't leave that lying there."

"It's not a lion, it's a Doomfang," said the Viking.

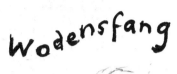

Wodensfang

I have to trust in the boy, and hope for the best.

I have to hope for the best.

"Perhaps I am a foolish, fond old dragon who never learns from my mistakes. But I have to believe that the humans and dragons are capable of living together."

"The fight goes on
for the Heroes of
the future…"

ABOUT THE AUTHOR

Cressida Cowell lives in London with her husband, Simon; their children, Maisie, Clementine, and Alexander; and two cats, Lily and Baloo. In addition to translating Hiccup's memoirs, she has written and illustrated picture books including *How to Be a Viking*, *Little Bo Peep's Library Book*, and *That Rabbit Belongs to Emily Brown*. Her website is www.cressidacowell.co.uk.

You don't *have* to read the Hiccup books in order.
But if you want to, this is the right order: